THE
BEACH
BANDIT

For Christie, my partner in crime —T.R.

Published in the United States by Random House Children's Books, a division of Penguin Random House LLC, 1745 Broadway, New York, NY 10019, and in Canada by Random House of Canada, a division of Penguin Random House Ltd., Toronto. Random House and the colophon are registered trademarks of Penguin Random House LLC.

ISBN 978-0-553-50847-5 (trade) — ISBN 978-0-375-97413-7 (lib. bdg.) — ISBN 978-1-101-93244-5 (ebook)

randomhousekids.com

Printed in the United States of America
10 9 8 7 6 5 4 3 2 1

Random House Children's Books supports the First Amendment and celebrates the right to read.

CHAPTER 1

"Come on!" Chelsea tugged Barbie's hand. She pulled her big sister past the dunes toward the ocean.

Barbie laughed. She playfully squeezed Chelsea's hand to slow her down. "What's the hurry? It's like you've never been to the beach before!"

"I hardly ever go with *all* my sisters," Chelsea explained, "and all our puppies!"

Stacie peeked over the mound of beach

gear she was carrying. "You mean you hardly ever have all your sisters to carry all your things!"

"Seriously!" Skipper said. Her arms were just as full. A bucket toppled off the top of a beach chair. It landed on Taffy, Barbie's sweet little puppy.

Woof! Taffy barked.

Chelsea came over. She picked up the bucket and gave Taffy a rub behind the ears. Then she ran to catch up with Barbie.

Barbie stopped by the lifeguard chair. "Let's set up here," she said. "I'm one of the lifeguards on duty today. I can keep an eye on the swimmers and talk to you!" Hanging out with her sisters made the day more fun.

"I can't take another step anyway," Skipper said as she collapsed on the sand.

Stacie flopped beside Skipper. Her puppy, Rookie, rushed over to lick her face.

"Yay!" Chelsea said. She sat down with the bucket and started to dig.

Honey barked happily. *"I'm just like Chelsea. We both love digging!"* she pointed out to the other pups.

Barbie bent down to pet Honey. The puppies were always barking back and forth. It was almost like they were talking!

Barbie shook her head and smiled to herself. What a silly idea—puppies couldn't talk, of course.

Next to them, Skipper and DJ scanned the beach. Skipper shaded her eyes. "Barbie, I think I see some of your friends," she said.

Barbie looked where Skipper was pointing. Sure enough, Ken and the twins, Ryan and Raquelle, were looking for a spot on the beach, too.

Barbie waved to them. "Want to set up near us?" she called.

"No thanks!" Raquelle called back.

"Okay!" Ryan yelled at the same time.

Ryan and Raquelle looked at each other.

"We'll be right there!" Ken added.

With a loud sigh, Raquelle walked with the guys across the sand. She looked as if she'd stepped off a runway. She was wearing four-inch wedge sandals, and her sequined beach wrap matched her sunglasses. She hadn't left her jewelry

at home either. She wore a diamond
necklace, a gold bracelet, and a ruby ring.

"You're really sparkly," Chelsea said.

Rookie sniffed and barked to his
siblings. *I think she forgot her tiara.*

"Be careful, sis," Ryan teased. "Someone

might run off with your jewels."

Chelsea looked around, wide-eyed. "For real? I'd better hide my flip-flops," she said. "They're covered in real sequins!"

"Your flip-flops are safe," Skipper said. "Unless the thief has really small feet."

Raquelle took off her necklace, bracelet, and ring and placed them in her bag. "Don't worry, Ryan," she told her brother. "I'm *always* careful. I'd never wear fine jewelry in the water." Then she put a hand on Ken's arm. "Ready for a swim?"

"Yes!" Chelsea answered.

"Definitely!" Ryan said. They all raced down to the water, even the puppies. Honey stopped at the edge of the surf. She wasn't sure about the waves. But the other puppies jumped right in!

Meanwhile, Barbie climbed onto the lifeguard chair and watched the swimmers.

Seagulls flew overhead.

A water-ice seller went past, pushing a chilled cart.

A Frisbee soared by, low to the ground.

A little boy started building a sand castle near his parents.

Other beachgoers came. They set up their picnics, blankets, and umbrellas.

Barbie made sure everyone was safe.

Her sisters, her friends, and the puppies had fun playing in the water.

Raquelle was the first to come back. She didn't want her fingertips to get wrinkly from the water.

"Have a nice swim?" Barbie asked.

"Lovely!" Raquelle said. "Too bad you have to work."

Barbie laughed. "I like being a lifeguard," she said. "Nothing is more important than keeping people safe!"

Raquelle wrung out her long hair. She put on fresh lip gloss. Then she looked at her bag. "Huh?" she said, frowning. "That's not where I remember leaving it." She turned her bag over onto her towel. Nothing came out.

Raquelle looked inside and let out a gasp.

"My jewelry!" she screamed. "It's gone!"

CHAPTER 2

"**G**one?" Barbie jumped down from the lifeguard stand. She called to another lifeguard to cover her watch.

"What's wrong? I heard a scream," Skipper said as she ran up to Barbie and Raquelle. "Are you okay, Raquelle?"

Raquelle shook her head. Her hand flew to her throat. She rubbed her neck where her diamond necklace had been less than an hour earlier.

"No," she said. "I'm not okay at all. Something terrible has happened!"

"I bet it was a shark!" Chelsea said.

"Did you get stung by a bee?" Stacie asked.

"Maybe she buried a bone and forgot where she put it," Rookie barked to the pups.

The other puppies nodded. That made perfect sense!

"It's worse!" Raquelle wailed. "My jewelry has been stolen!" She showed everyone the empty bag.

"Stolen?" Chelsea dove toward her towel. Seconds later, she held up her sequined flip-flops. "Phew!" she said. "The thief must have missed these!"

Honey barked and wagged her tail. She liked the flip-flops, too. They were tasty to chew on.

Skipper frowned. "Barbie was here the whole time," she said. "She would have seen someone with Raquelle's bag. Right, Barbie?"

"I was watching the water," Barbie said. "But I'm sure I would have seen a thief." She looked again at Raquelle's bag. The puppies were sniffing around it. Barbie had an idea.

"Raquelle," Barbie began, "you said something when you went to pick up your bag. You said, 'That's not where I remember leaving it.'"

Raquelle nodded slowly. "I did say that."
She frowned. "I had left my bag standing
up. But when I came back, it was on its
side."

"Can you show me?" Barbie asked.

Raquelle thought for a moment. Then
she placed the bag on one side, facing
toward the dunes.

Barbie looked at it. Her eye traveled
up the beach. There! In the sand, ten feet
away, was a yellow Frisbee.

Barbie clapped her hands. "I saw that
Frisbee fly past the lifeguard stand,"

she said. "Maybe it hit your bag . . . and knocked it over. Maybe your jewelry fell out, into the sand!"

"Of course!" Raquelle said. She flipped her long hair over her shoulder. "I should have thought of that!"

Raquelle pushed at the sand with her foot. "I just had my nails done," she said. "I don't want to mess them up digging in the sand."

"I'll do it!" Chelsea said, holding a shovel up high. "I'll be a pirate, digging for buried treasure!"

CHAPTER 3

Chelsea dug in a big circle around the bag.

The puppies decided to help. *"I'll take the right side,"* Taffy barked. *"Honey, you take the left."*

"Left?" Honey turned in a circle. *"Which way is that?"*

The four puppies set to work, sending up sprays of sand.

Chelsea and Stacie found seashells and

seaweed. They found pretty rocks. But no diamonds.

"Did you find them?" Raquelle asked.

"Not yet," Stacie said. She had put all the shells and rocks in a pile to one side. She picked up a purple-and-white shell from the top. "This shell is really pretty, though."

Raquelle sniffed. "Hardly!"

Honey sniffed the shell. She licked it. *"Ugh. It sure looks better than it tastes!"* she barked to the pups.

Barbie gave Raquelle a hug. "Don't

worry," Barbie said. "Your diamonds will turn up."

A little boy stopped in front of Stacie. He was carrying a pail of water from the ocean. "Can I have that shell for my pirate sand castle?" he asked.

"Sure," Stacie said.

"Thanks!" The boy raced off. Water slopped out of his bucket as he ran.

"See? *He* thinks I found treasure!" Stacie said.

"If the diamonds aren't in the sand," Skipper said, "where did they go?"

A seagull glided by and landed on the pile of sand. It flapped its wings.

"Shoo!" Chelsea said. She waved her hands at the seagull.

Barbie hid a smile. She liked seagulls. They reminded her of beach days and sunshine.

The puppies leaped into the air and barked at the seagull.

Stacie turned to see what had gotten them so worked up. "Hey!" She jumped to her feet. The bird took off. "That gull had something in its beak. Something shiny!"

"Shiny like jewelry?" Raquelle asked.

"Maybe!" Stacie said. Her eyes followed the seagull through the sky. "We need to find out what he's got!"

Stacie ran down the beach after the seagull. After a second, Skipper and the four puppies followed her.

The seagull landed on the beach again.

"Okay," Stacie whispered to Skipper. "Let's corner him!"

Stacie sneaked toward the seagull. She was getting closer. The puppies were right on her heels. When Stacie was just a few feet away, DJ pounced!

"Oh no!" Stacie said. She lunged forward.

But the seagull lifted off the sand and flew away.

Stacie landed flat on her stomach. She pounded the sand with her fist. "So close!" she said.

"Look!" Skipper said to her sister. "It landed again!"

Skipper and Stacie ran to where the seagull had settled. They closed in on the bird. With a grunt, Stacie reached out. The

seagull squawked, its beak opening wide, and flew off.

"Argggh!" Stacie said.

"Wait," Skipper said. She pointed to the sand. Something lay there, shining in the sunshine. "It dropped something!"

CHAPTER 4

Skipper plucked the shiny thing from the sand.

"What is it?" Stacie asked. She leaned in close. "A ruby ring?"

Taffy stuck her nose in, too. She wanted to see!

Skipper opened her fist. In her palm was . . . a red bottle cap. "I'm not sure Raquelle will want a Grapeberry Tea cap instead of her ring."

Stacie giggled and covered her mouth.

Stacie, Skipper, and the puppies returned to the lifeguard chair to tell Barbie and Raquelle the news. "The seagull's not the thief," Skipper said. She showed Raquelle the bottle cap.

"Ooh, can I have that?" The sand castle boy was back with another pail of water.

"Sure!" Skipper said.

Barbie watched the little boy run off toward his parents. His sand castle was getting big. He had even dug a moat around it.

Barbie turned back to Skipper and Stacie. "It's okay," she told them. "We found another clue!" She pointed toward Raquelle's towel. Narrow tracks cut through the sand next to it, where Chelsea hadn't dug.

"Come on, puppies," DJ called. *"Let's check them out!"*

"Huh," Stacie said. She watched the puppies sniff the tracks. "What made them?"

"I remember seeing a water-ice seller go by," Barbie said. "She had a wheeled cart. Maybe she ran over the jewelry by accident. Maybe it got caught on a tire!"

Raquelle crossed her arms. "Or maybe she *took* them. They are beautiful, after all."

"I'm sure it's all a mistake," Barbie said. She couldn't believe anyone would take the jewelry on purpose.

"We can find out," Stacie said, taking out her trusty magnifying glass. She was always ready to solve a mystery. "Let's follow the trail!"

"I need to patrol the beach anyway,"

Barbie said. "I'll just check in with Jack to make sure he's covered." On her cell phone, she called the other lifeguard.

"I'll stay here," Raquelle said as she struck a movie star pose on her beach towel and put her sunglasses on.

"Noses to the ground, pups!" Taffy barked. They followed the trail with Stacie, Barbie, Chelsea, and Skipper behind them. The cart trail swerved around a beach towel and a volleyball court. It veered close to the surf, then back up the beach.

"I see her!" Stacie yelled. About twenty

feet ahead of them, the water-ice seller had stopped near a family. Stacie took off, running across the sand.

Skipper looked at Barbie. Barbie looked at Skipper. Chelsea looked at both of them. They all broke into a run. The puppies took off after them.

"Excuse me," Stacie said when they caught up to the water-ice seller. "May I check your tires?"

"My tires?" The girl laughed. "Sure. Knock yourself out."

Stacie dropped to the sand. She studied

the tires with her magnifying glass. Rookie put his nose next to them, too. Nothing was caught on the axle. Nothing was stuck in the treads.

Stacie sat on her heels and sighed. "Rats! I was hoping for diamonds."

The girl brightened. "You should have just asked," she said. She patted the side of the cart. "I have the diamonds right in here!"

CHAPTER 5

Barbie's heart beat faster. "You do?"

The girl nodded. She opened the lid of her cart and reached inside. Skipper held her breath. Stacie stood on her tiptoes to see inside. Chelsea squeezed Barbie's hand.

The girl pulled out two water-ice cones. "Diamond pops," she said. "They're our best sellers!"

Skipper groaned. "Diamond pops?" she repeated.

Chelsea jumped up and down. "Hooray! Diamond pops! Can I have one?" she asked Barbie.

Barbie laughed. "I think you like these better than *real* diamonds," she said.

Chelsea shrugged. "They sure taste better!"

Barbie bought each of her sisters a diamond pop. Then she remembered her friend. "Should we get one for Raquelle?" she asked.

Skipper laughed. "I don't think Raquelle would find it funny."

Barbie bought some cold water for the puppies. She poured it into a paper cup. They lapped at it happily.

"It's hot in the sun," Taffy barked.

"Yeah, especially when you have fur!" Honey added.

Slurping the cones, the sisters walked back toward the lifeguard stand.

"Look! Ken and Ryan are back from swimming," Stacie said.

The guys were sitting on the sand next to Raquelle, listening to her explain about her missing jewelry.

"I just know someone stole it!" Raquelle finished.

Ken looked puzzled. "So who is the beach bandit?"

"I hope you learned your lesson, sis. I knew this would happen one day!" Ryan crossed his arms and frowned at Raquelle. "Who told you to be careful?"

Raquelle sighed. She blew a strand of hair from in front of her eyes. "You did, dear brother."

"Who told you someone might steal your jewelry?" Ryan asked.

Raquelle pouted. "You, brother dear."

Ryan smirked. "And who—"

With a gasp, Skipper jumped up. "Wait a minute!" she said. "Ryan, did you take

Raquelle's jewelry to teach her a lesson?"

The puppies clustered around Ryan's feet and barked to each other.

"Ryan?" DJ barked. *"A beach bandit?"*

"No!" Taffy shook her head. *"He wouldn't do that!"*

"He smells too good," Honey added.

"I didn't take the diamonds. I swear!" Ryan said. He took a step back. He didn't notice a beach chair right behind him. He stumbled and fell over it—backward!

CHAPTER 6

Ryan landed with a thud on the sand. "Hey!" he said. "Who put that there?"

"Man down, man down!" DJ barked.

The contents of Ryan's pockets had fallen into the sand. A lip balm and a set of keys fell from one pocket. A guitar pick and a library card fell from the other. No necklace. No bracelet. No ring.

Taffy shook her head and barked to the pups. *"Told you he didn't do it."*

"You brought your library card to the beach?" Stacie teased.

The little boy with the bucket walked by again. "Cool guitar pick!" he said. "Can I have it?"

"It's yours," Ryan said. He handed the pick to the kid.

The kid looked at the keys. "Those, too?" he asked.

Ryan laughed. He put his keys away. "Nice try," he said. "Maybe in twelve years you'll know what to do with a car!"

Barbie gave the boy a big smile. "Your sand castle is wonderful!" she said.

The boy had built high walls and dug a moat. He'd made ten turrets. Each was topped with sand drippings and decorated with shells. The red bottle cap had a place of honor on the front turret. Just below it was a super-sparkly stone.

Barbie took another look. That stone—she hadn't noticed it before. "Wait a second . . . ," she said.

Barbie knelt next to the castle. "Princess cut," she muttered. "About two carats. Clarity—flawless. This isn't a rock. It's a diamond!"

"A diamond?" Ryan and Ken echoed.

"A diamond!" Chelsea squealed.

Barbie pulled on the stone. A thin chain with the diamond came free from the turret. She held the diamond up to the sun.

"It's pirate treasure!" the little boy said.

"Where did you get it?" Barbie asked the little boy.

"Over there." He pointed to the sand . . . next to Raquelle's bag!

Stacie leaned forward. "Did you find anything else?"

"Sure!" The boy dashed to the back of the castle. He pulled off a gold bracelet and a ruby ring. "I found these, too. They're my pirate treasure!"

"Pirate treasure," Chelsea. "I was digging in the wrong place!"

"Or in the right place," Barbie said,

"but at the wrong time. I think the Frisbee knocked over the bag. The diamonds fell out. And he found them while he was looking for shells. That's why I didn't see anyone go into Raquelle's bag."

"My jewelry—at last!" Raquelle said. She reached for her jewelry. But the little boy pulled them away.

"Uh-uh," he said. "You can't have my treasure."

"It's not *your* treasure," Raquelle said. "It's *mine*!"

Ryan laughed. "Sis, you should know

better than to come between a pirate and his treasure."

Barbie wanted to laugh, too, but Raquelle looked ready to burst. Barbie had to find a way to get the jewelry back . . . and keep the boy happy. But how?

"I know!" Barbie cried. She whispered into Stacie's ear. Stacie listened and nodded. She and Rookie ran down the beach.

Soon they returned, and Stacie handed something to Barbie.

Barbie crouched down next to the

little boy. "I'll trade you," she said, "for something better than your treasure. It's way yummier." She winked at Chelsea and pulled a water ice from behind her back. "A diamond pop!"

The boy's eyes widened. "A diamond pop? Hooray!" He tossed Raquelle's jewelry over his shoulder and grabbed the water ice.

Raquelle shrieked. She dove after her jewelry. One by one, she dug the pieces out of the sand. Necklace. Bracelet. Ring. She didn't even seem to care about her nails.

With a relieved sigh, she put the jewelry on. "I'm never taking these off again," she vowed.

"Not even for a diamond pop?" Barbie asked.

"Some people like diamond pops," Raquelle said with a nod at Chelsea. "But *real* diamonds are this girl's best friend!"

"Well, it looks like that mystery's solved," Barbie said, picking up her towel and shaking out the sand.

"Can we solve another one?" Chelsea asked, holding up the magnifying glass.

"I think I'm getting the hang of this."

Stacie's stomach growled loudly. "Can we solve the mystery of what's for lunch? I'm hungry."

"This sounds like a case for the Super Awesome Chelsea Roberts Mystery Club!" Chelsea said.

"Hey!" Skipper said, laughing. "What about us?"

"How about the Sisters Mystery Club?" Barbie suggested. "And how about we try that new sandwich place on the boardwalk for lunch?"

"Deal!" Chelsea, Skipper, and Stacie said.

As the sisters walked toward the boardwalk, they imagined all the fun mysteries they would solve together and the amazing adventures they would share.